# THE SEVENTH DAY

Deborah Bodin Cohen

Illustrated by *Melanie Hall*

KAR-BEN
PUBLISHING

KAR-BEN PUBLISHING, INC.
A division of Lerner Publishing Group
241 First Avenue North
Minneapolis, MN 55401 U.S.A.
1-800-4KARBEN

Website address: www.karben.com

Library of Congress Cataloging-in-Publication Data

Cohen, Deborah Bodin, 1968–
    The seventh day / by Deborah Bodin Cohen ; illustrated by Melanie Hall.
        p.   cm.
    Summary: Like a potter, a painter, and a musician, God creates the earth and what dwells there,
then celebrates having finished his work by sharing a cup of grape juice with the boy and girl he
made in his image and resting on the first Shabbat.
    ISBN: 0–929371–24–0 (lib. bdg. : alk. paper)
    ISBN: 1–58013–125–5 (pbk. : alk. paper)
    [1. Creation—Fiction. 2. God—Fiction. 3. Sabbath—Fiction.] I. Hall, Melanie W., ill.
II. Title.
PZ7.C6623Se  2005
[E]—dc22                                                                      2004004945

Manufactured in the United States of America
1 2 3 4 5 6 – DP – 10 09 08 07 06 05

*To Arianna Shira* —D.B.C.

*To my cousins, Paula and George Meyer,
and Rose and Ron Jackson, with love.* —M.H.

*For six days, God worked.*

*For six nights, God didn't stop to rest.*

*L*ike a potter, God formed desert canyons and riverbeds. God's hands pressed against the earth and molded snow-topped mountains and bright green valleys.

*Like a painter, God colored the sky crystal blue and sunburst yellow. God took in deep breaths and blew out fluffy white clouds. God painted night deep black. And God drew silver stars and a purple moon in the night sky.*

*Like a musician, God sang out the sounds of water flowing over rocks, thunder cracking, and echoes in seashells.*

God looked at Creation. "It is good," said God.
But God was not satisfied. And although
God was tired, God kept working.

*L*ike a potter, God formed
pink coral in the sea and
moss-covered tree trunks
in the forest.

Like a painter, God colored the leopard's spots, the zebra's stripes, and the panda's black-and-white patches.

*L*ike a musician, God sang out the sounds of lions roaring, owls hooting, and dolphins splashing through the waves.

God's palm opened and released field mice, woolly sheep, and kangaroos. God gently placed fish into the sea and ladybugs on the ground. God blessed all the creatures of the world.

"They are good," said God,
with a little more excitement.
But God still was not satisfied.
And although very tired, God
kept working.

*A*t noon on the sixth day, God called out,
"Let's make a boy and girl in our image."
Like a potter, God molded their necks, fingernails,
and the spaces between their toes.

*L*ike a painter, God colored their eyes, lips, and hair and drew rosy brown freckles on their faces.

Like a musician, God breathed
voices into their throats and tickled
laughs into their bellies and
prayers into their souls.

*L*ate in the afternoon on the sixth day, God looked
at the boy and girl. At last, God was satisfied.
"Creation is very good," God called out with joy.
"The world is finished. I can finally rest. It is time
for Shabbat." God watched the sun slowly fall.
"Let's celebrate," God called out to all the creatures.

Like a potter, God stretched out a hand, plucked a bunch of juicy grapes from the vineyard, and squeezed them tight. Sweet purple juice ran through God's fingers. God caught the juice in golden kiddush cups—one cup for the boy, one cup for the girl.

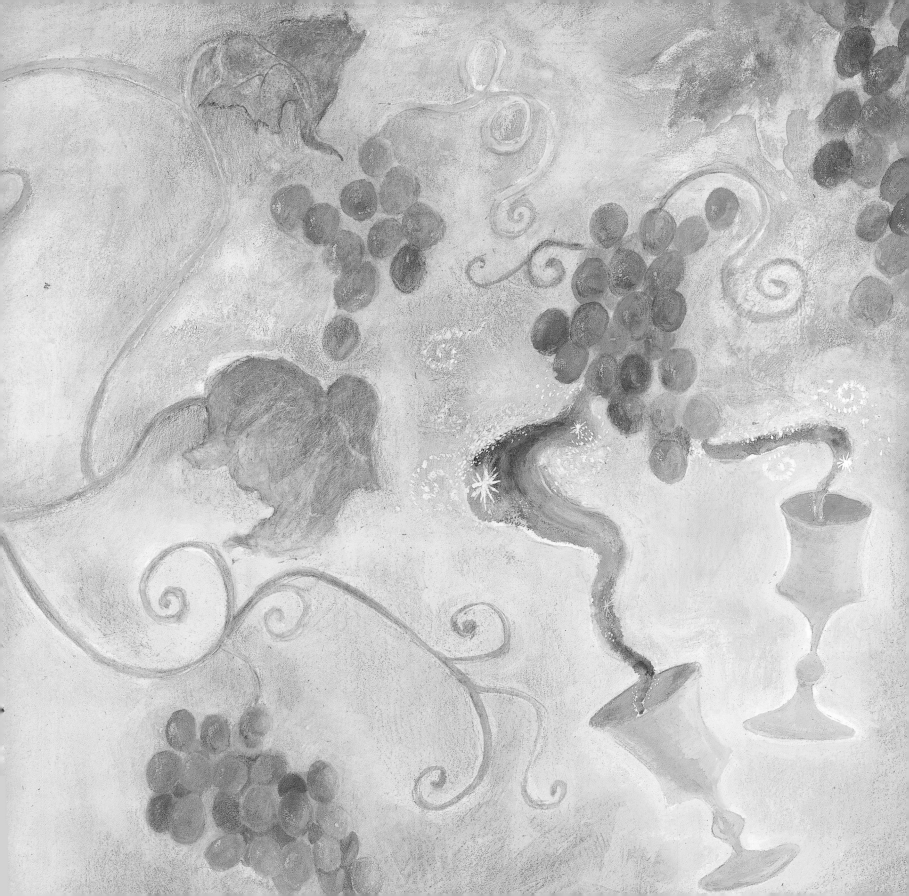

Like a painter, God swept a hand, covered
with grape juice, across the early evening sky.
The purple juice mixed with the orange and
pink rays of the setting sun.

All the
creatures
looked at
the sunset.

*Like a musician, God blessed Shabbat and filled the day with song and prayer.*

*The boy and the girl joined in.*

"Blessed are You, our God, for creating the fruit of the vine.

Blessed are You, our God, for the gift of Shabbat,

a day to remember and celebrate all that You have created."

*And all living creatures, great and small, called out,*
*"L'Chayim—To Life!"*